The Ballet
Class Mystery

The Adventures of Callie Ann

Summer Surprise
The Ballet Class Mystery

The Ballet Class Mystery

Shannon Mason Leppard

BETHANY HOUSE PUBLISHERS
MINNEAPOLIS, MINNESOTA 55438

Published by Bethany House Publishers
A Ministry of Bethany Fellowship, Inc.
11300 Hampshire Avenue South
Minneapolis, Minnesota 55438

Printed in the United States of America.

Library of Congress Cataloging-in-Publication Data

Leppard, Shannon Mason.
    The ballet class mystery / Shannon Mason Leppard.
        p.   cm. — (The adventures of Callie Ann ; book 2)
    Summary: As she slowly gets used to her new home, nine-
year-old Callie finds herself absorbed in trying to discover
the identity of the mysterious boy she sees dancing at the
studio where she takes classes.
    ISBN 1–55661–814–X (pbk.)
    [1. Friendship—Fiction. 2. Family life—Fiction.
3. Christian life—Fiction.] I. Title. II. Series: Leppard,
Shannon Mason. Adventures of Callie Ann ; book 2.
PZ7.L5565Bal   1996
[Fic]—dc21   96–45834
                                               CIP
                                               AC

For Sara Mason Morris, my mother.
Thank you for being there.
I love you.

Also, for Dan Mason and Yvonne Mason,
my brother and sister.
I love you more than words can say.
Y'all are the best!

SHANNON MASON LEPPARD grew up in a small town in South Carolina, where summer days were spent under the shade of an old weeping willow tree and winters under the quilting frames of her grandmother. Shannon brings her flair for drama and make-believe to THE ADVENTURES OF CALLIE ANN, her first series with Bethany House. She and her husband, Donn, make their home in North Carolina along with their two teenage daughters.

Chapter One

"Callie! Meghan!" Callie's mom called from the kitchen. "You two need to get up now. Meghan's mom will be here in only two hours."

"Oh no, it can't be Saturday already!" Callie Ann Davies rolled over and took most of the sunflower quilt with her.

"C'mon, Cal. We have to get going if you want to show me the bell tower and the Cornelius school again before my mom comes." Meghan Johnson yanked the quilt back.

That got Callie moving. She tugged even harder on the quilt, and soon Callie and Meghan were in an all-out tug-of-war.

They were still playing with the quilt when the second call came up from the kitchen. "I guess we'd better get moving. Where are the cats?" Callie looked around the room.

"I think David let them out early this morning. At least I think it was David. All I saw was a lot of blond hair. Could have been your dad." Meghan pulled on the same jean shorts she wore the day before.

"Must have been David. Daddy had to go to the hospital this morning to visit the Mason twins."

A third warning came up from the kitchen as Callie was tying her shoes. "Girls, this is it! Move it, or I'll have to come up and get you both."

Callie knew her mom was in a hurry this morning. As soon as Meghan and her mom left, Callie and her mom had to visit Miss Karen's School of Ballet in Statesville. *Just what I want to do*, Callie thought to herself, *start over at a new dance class*.

Callie's family had just moved from Greenville to Cornelius, where her daddy was the new pastor. Meghan had been Callie's best friend in Greenville. She had come to visit as a surprise for Callie's birthday. But now it was time for Meghan to go home.

Downstairs, Mom had made Callie's favorite for breakfast—peanut butter toast and milk.

"What are you two going to do today?" Mom asked as she sat down at the table with the girls.

"We're going over to the school—and to see the bell tower again," Callie answered, a big grin on her face. She was getting used to living in Cornelius. She even liked it—a little.

"Are we going to ask Jason to come with us?" Meghan asked.

"I guess we can, if you want to." Callie still wasn't sure why Meghan wanted Jason Alexander to go everywhere with them. She thought that maybe—just maybe—Meghan liked Jason. But he was a *boy*!

"Yes, I'd really like that. If you don't mind." Meghan was blushing now.

"Fine by me. I mean, if you want a *boy* to go with us, I guess it'd be OK." Callie gave Meghan a strange look. Had her best friend gone over the deep end about a boy? Meghan sure had changed. She didn't even like fishing anymore. "I'll call him after we eat," Callie said.

"Great! I'll just run up and change while you

finish your breakfast." Meghan had a giant smile on her face.

"Change what?" Callie asked. Now she knew for sure Meghan had flipped. Changing clothes to go for a bike ride with a *boy*!

"I just want to look nice when Mom gets here, that's all. It's not like I want to look good for Jason or anything." Meghan sounded mad.

"Whatever, Meg. Just go do whatever," Callie said sadly. Meghan liked Jason, that's all there was to it.

While Meghan was changing, Callie called Jason.

"Sure, I'll come. Are you two over your little fit?" he asked.

"What fit are you talking about, Jason Alexander? Meghan and I don't have fits." Callie looked around the kitchen to see if her mom was listening.

"You know, the one the other day. You said Meghan liked me, and she said she didn't," Jason answered.

"Well, just so you'll know, Mr. Alexander, she does like you!" Callie said.

"Get real, Cal. Meghan is just like you. Y'all

hate boys, and you know it. I have to go now so I can get my bike. See ya in a few." With that, Jason hung up the phone, leaving a very mad Callie on the other end.

As soon as Meghan came down, she and Callie went out the back door to get their bikes. Jason was coming across the backyard with Jack, his all-white cat, behind him.

"Oh, look, Callie," Meghan gushed, "Jason brought his cat."

"Oh, brother. You act like you've never seen a cat before. If you'll remember, we both have cats," Callie teased.

"I'm just trying to be nice. That's more than I can say for you," Meghan said as she crossed the yard to meet Jason.

Callie was about to say something when she saw a car pulling into the driveway. "Who drives a gray Honda?" Callie yelled.

Meghan turned to look at the car. "Mom? But she said she was coming around lunch. Why is she here now?"

"Hi, Mrs. Johnson. You're early," Callie said as she, Meghan, and Jason went to the driveway.

"I know, and I'm sorry. It's just that I need to

stop at the office in Charlotte before we go back. Then we have to stop in at the main office when we get to Greenville," Mrs. Johnson said as she gave Meghan a hug. "Did you have a good time? Why are you so dressed up?"

"No reason," Meghan answered, looking around.

I bet she's hoping Jason notices, Callie thought.

"I'll go get my mom, Mrs. Johnson. I'll be right back." Callie ran to the back door of the house. Mom was already coming out by the time Callie got there. "Mom, Meghan's mom is here."

"I saw. I'm sorry y'all won't have time to take that ride you wanted to," Mom said as they made their way around the house. "But now we'll have time to do something with your hair before we go to dance class."

Great, Callie thought. *First she makes me go to dance class. Now she wants to mess with my hair!* She brushed her curly hair back off her face. Callie had lots of wild red hair that was often out of control. *Best thing to do with all this is to put it in a ponytail.* That way Mom wouldn't try to blow-dry it again. Blow-drying only made it wilder.

"Girls, you need to go get Meghan's things. And look for Mr. Kitty so Meghan can take him home. David let him and Miss Kitty out this morning on his way to Jenni's house." Callie's mom looked around for any sign of the big black cats. They were brother and sister.

"I'll look for the cats." Jason headed off across the yard. While he looked for the cats, Meghan and Callie went into the house to get together Meghan's things.

"Callie, are you mad at me?" Meghan asked as she packed her bag. She wouldn't look at her friend.

"In a way, I guess. I mean, you came to visit *me*. But all we've done is ride with Jason, or sit under the pecan tree with Jason." Callie sat down on the bed.

"I'm sorry, Cal, but Jason *is* really cute. I don't think he likes me, though. He'd rather just hang around with you. Maybe he likes *you*." Meghan sounded smug.

"Meghan Marie Johnson, Jason is a BOY. And I really don't like boys right now. It's hard enough living in a new town—and now I have a new dance class, too. You're just mad because he doesn't like you."

With that, Callie turned and walked out of her room. She almost ran into Jason in the hallway. "Jason! How long have you been in the house?" Callie asked, surprised.

"Long enough. You and Meghan shouldn't fight, Callie. We can all be friends. You don't need to fight with her over me." Jason had a huge grin on his face.

"Fight over you!" Meghan yelled as she came into the hallway. "Why in the world do you think we'd fight over you? You're a BOY!" Her face was really red.

Callie was laughing so hard, she forgot to ask if Jason had found the cats.

"Having a good time?" Callie's mom asked as they came downstairs. She must have heard all the laughing.

Suddenly, Callie remembered Meghan was leaving. "Oh, Meg, I'm going to miss you so much! Are you sure you and your mom don't want to move up here?" Callie hugged Meghan tightly.

"Please don't do that, Callie. I'll cry, and Mom will be upset. . . . Oh, Callie, I'll miss you, too." Meghan cried into Callie's hair. "Why did y'all have to move away?"

"I've asked that a million times. And I always get the same answer. This is what God wanted Daddy to do. Maybe someday we'll move back home to Greenville." Callie dried her eyes on her shirt-sleeve.

"Well, Meg, are you ready?" Meghan's mom called from the back porch. "I have Mr. Kitty in the car."

"I have to go now. But I'll write. And you can come down when you visit your grandmama." Meghan hugged Callie again.

"I'll write, too. And Mom said I could call sometime if we don't talk too long. I miss you a lot already," Callie called as Meghan walked to the car.

Callie, her mom, and Jason waved as Mrs. Johnson and Meghan backed out of the driveway.

" 'Bye, Callie! I love you lots!" Meghan yelled as their car went down the street. " 'Bye."

I wonder when I'll get to see her again, Callie thought as she wiped her eyes again.

15

Chapter Two

"I can't believe she had to leave so soon. I wish we could go back home," Callie said as they turned back to the yard.

"Oh, brother, here we go again," Jason said. "You *are* home. Remember me? I live next door. You know, I'm the one you like so well." Jason raced across the backyard toward his house.

"Oh yeah? I'll get you, Jason Alexander!" Callie ran after Jason. "You know I don't like you. Well—I do like you, but not like that. You're a BOY!"

"Don't be gone too long," Mom called as Callie chased Jason across the yard. "You have to get dressed to go to dance class."

"How did I know that was coming?" Callie

said as she sat down beside Jason under the huge pecan tree.

"Well, you just might like the class. I bet you'll meet some of the girls we'll go to school with this fall." Jason picked up a pecan.

"Do you know anybody who takes ballet?" Callie asked.

"Not really. But I'm sure somebody does," Jason said. "Look, I've got to go cut grass. I'll see you after you get back from Miss Karen's." He stood up and jogged back to his yard.

"Miss Kitty, I guess you and I have to go in. I need to get dressed for ballet class now. Come on." Callie pulled the big black cat up to her. "Boy, are you ever getting heavy!"

❧❧❧

Callie's mom was trying to put Callie's hair up in a bun when the phone rang. Callie ran to answer it.

"Hello?"

"Hello, is this Callie?" a woman's voice said.

"Yes, ma'am," Callie replied.

"This is Karen Baker, your new ballet teacher. I just wanted to let you know that you could come early. You can look around before your class starts, if you'd like."

"Great," Callie said. "We'll be there in just a little while. Thank you." She put the phone down and turned to her mom. "That was Miss Karen. She said we could come early if we wanted to."

"Great. Let's try to at least pull your hair back first," Mom said with a smile.

"Maybe we could just cut it all off," Callie said.

"Oh no! Remember what happened last time we did that? You cried for a week! And we *really* couldn't do anything with it then." Mom pulled Callie's hair back with a headband.

"I guess we're ready," Callie said as she went down the steps to the kitchen. "Miss Kitty, you have to stay here until I get back. Then I'll let you go out to play with Jack." Callie picked up the black cat and put her on the chair in the kitchen.

Mom and Callie waved to Jason as they backed out of the drive. *Here we go*, Callie thought. *Starting over. . . .*

☙☙☙

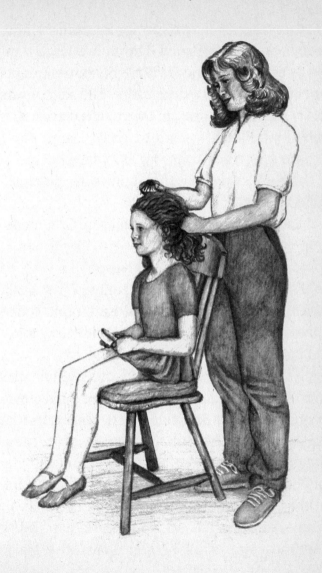

Mom and Callie pulled up in front of Miss Karen's School of Ballet. Through a large window, Callie could see several girls in pink tights dancing all around a large room. The school was not as big as the one in Greenville. At least, it didn't look like it.

"Are you ready to go in?" Mom asked.

"I guess. Are you sure I have to do this?" Callie whined.

"Callie Ann, you loved ballet in Greenville. What makes you think you won't like it here?" Mom looked at Callie and frowned.

"I didn't say I don't like ballet. I just don't want to start over. What if Miss Karen puts me in a class for little kids?" Callie asked, feeling sorry for herself.

"Nobody said you would be, Callie. Miss Karen will look at the records we have from Greenville. She'll see what class you fit into at her school. It'll be fine. You'll see." Her mom hugged Callie close.

Once inside the school, Callie couldn't pick out the teacher. Miss Mary, the teacher back in Greenville, was tall and had dark hair. Here everybody was a lot shorter than Miss Mary.

Then a small lady with blond hair came across the room, smiling.

"Hello, I'm Karen Baker. You must be Callie Davies." The blond lady reached out to shake hands with Callie. "It will be so nice to have you in class."

"Hi, I'm Sara Davies, Callie's mom." Mom held her hand out to Miss Karen.

As the two women talked, Callie looked around. Nobody looked nine. *This must be a beginners' class,* Callie thought to herself.

The school was a lot bigger than Callie thought it was. There were two big rooms, and it looked like four smaller ones off to the side. *How many girls take dance here?* she wondered.

"Would you like to look around, Callie?" Miss Karen asked.

"Sure. Would you mind?" Callie answered, remembering that Mom had told her to always mind her manners.

"Not at all, Callie. This is your school, too. And I want you to feel right at home," Miss Karen said.

"Can I ask you a question?" Callie asked.

"You sure can." Miss Karen smiled.

"How old is this group? I mean, this isn't my class, is it?" Callie asked.

"Oh my, no, Callie. These are the five-year-olds," Miss Karen answered. "Your class doesn't begin until one o'clock. These little ladies have about twenty more minutes."

Callie smiled at Miss Karen. She really wasn't much taller than Callie. "Thank you. I'll just look around now."

Callie wandered through a short hallway and peeked into one of the smaller rooms. There she saw a little boy with red hair—just like hers! But he was dancing all by himself. *That's strange,* she thought. *Why isn't he out here with all the others?*

Just then Callie heard her mom calling. "Coming, Mom," she called back. When she turned back to the small room, the boy wasn't there anymore. Callie peeked into all the rooms as she went back down the short hall that led to the large room. But she didn't see the boy anywhere.

Where did he go? Callie thought. *He just disappeared!*

Chapter Three

Callie was still wondering about the boy as Mom handed Callie her bag. "You need to change your shoes for class now."

"But, Mom—" Callie started.

"No time for buts, Miss Callie. Your class starts in just a few minutes. Go on now."

"OK, but I really want to ask a question," Callie muttered as she turned to go into the dressing room.

"Ask me later, Callie. Hurry now, or you won't be ready when the others get here."

Just as Callie went to the dressing room, she saw him again. This time he smiled at her and walked into a room at the back of the school. *Who is that boy?* Callie thought. *I'll ask Mom if she saw him when I finish*.

By the time Callie got her ballet shoes on and joined her class, there were four other girls in the room. Miss Karen was talking with them.

"Callie, come meet the other girls," Miss Karen called to her. "This is Natalie West and her cousin Jordan Moore. They live in Davidson. Then we have Emilee Brown and Leslie Herndon, who live in Cornelius. And here comes the last of your class—Brandi Baker, my niece. Girls, this is Callie Davies."

"Hello," they all said at once.

Jordan Moore moved away from the other girls and said, "I hope you like it here. We just have a small group. But it's lots of fun. We're the oldest group Miss Karen has at this school. She also teaches in Charlotte."

"You mean this is it? Only six of us? Great!" Callie looked around. *Wow. At home there were twenty girls in my ballet class*, Callie thought. *Now I have lots of room to really move*.

"Yep, this is it," Natalie West said as she walked up. "Have you been here long?"

"We moved to Cornelius in May. My dad is the pastor of a local church there." Callie turned to look at Natalie. She was really pretty, with blond hair and dark blue eyes. She was a lot taller than most of the other girls. *She must be older,* Callie thought.

Callie wanted to ask if anyone knew who the little boy was, but Miss Karen called the class to order.

"Ready, ladies?" Miss Karen said so loudly that Callie jumped. "My goodness, I forgot where I am. I have to talk that loud in Charlotte because the class has thirty girls. Sorry, ladies."

Callie smiled. *I really think I'm going to like it here. But I sure want to know who that little boy is!*

The class danced about an hour, and then Miss Karen said everyone could do the woolly wiggle.

"What is that?" Callie asked Emilee.

"Oh, it's great! You dance any way you want to. Miss Karen puts on music from the sixties, and we all just get the woolly wiggles." Emilee flashed a big smile at Callie. "Come on, you'll have lots of fun."

Callie stood back for a few minutes until she

just couldn't help herself. She got the woolly wiggles, too!

When Mom came in, she laughed so hard that there were tears in her eyes. Then Miss Karen told Callie to give her mom the woolly wiggles. Callie ran to her mom and pulled her onto the dance floor.

"Oh, look, Callie! Your mom has the wiggles, too!" Brandi laughed. "My mom loves to do this with me."

"Yeah, and she's good at it," Jordan answered as she whirled past Callie and Brandi.

"OK, girls, time to unwiggle now," Miss Karen said. "We've had a great class. I'll see all of you on Monday. Callie, it's great having you with us. Love you all." She blew them all kisses.

"Oh, Mom, I had a great time! I really did! Thank you for getting me to come." Callie sailed into her mom's arms. "I'll be right back after I change."

With that, she ran with the other girls into the dressing room to change.

Callie was the last one out. As she came down the hall, there he was again—the little boy with red hair. And he was still dancing all by

himself. *That's really strange,* Callie thought. *I'll ask Miss Karen about him.*

" 'Bye, Callie, see you on Monday," Natalie called as she went out to meet her mom.

"Mom," Callie said as she came back into the big room. "Did you see that little boy with hair the same color as mine? He's dancing all by himself in the room over there." But by the time Callie and her mom went to look, the little boy wasn't there.

"No, sweetie, I didn't see anybody. Are you sure there wasn't anyone with him?" Mom asked.

"I didn't see anybody," Callie answered. "Where is Miss Karen? I'll ask her." Callie went to look for her.

But Miss Karen had already left to teach another dance class.

"I guess I'll just have to wait until Monday to ask her," Callie sighed.

Chapter Four

On the way home, Callie had an idea. She could ask Jason! He knew most of the boys in their class at school. Maybe he would know who the little boy was.

As soon as Mom and Callie pulled up in the drive, Callie saw Jason and his mom. They were getting into their red Jeep.

"Hey, Jason! Wait! I need to ask you something," Callie yelled as she ran across the backyard to his house.

"Later, Callie. We'll be back around six or so. We have to meet my dad in Charlotte. 'Bye." Jason waved out the car window as they backed out of the driveway.

Later, later—that's all I get, Callie thought to

herself. *I really want to know who that little boy is at ballet class. But I guess now I'll have to wait.*

Walking back to her house, Callie hoped that Jason would know who the boy was. If not, she'd have to wait until Monday—but Monday was so far away!

As Callie reached the porch, Mom came out the back door.

"Callie, Miss Karen was just on the phone," she said. "She wants to know if you'd like to dance in a show the nursing home in Statesville is having Monday afternoon. She said you could practice a few dances in class, then go to the nursing home and do the show." Mom brushed the hair out of Callie's eyes.

"Sure. I'd love to do that," Callie said. "She must have thought I did OK today, otherwise she wouldn't have called. Don't you think so, Mom?" Callie looked hopefully at her mom.

"I'm sure she loved your dancing," Mom said. "And I loved doing the woolly wiggle." She shook herself all over.

Callie and her mom laughed and wiggled all the way into the house.

"Do you want a snack before I clean up the kitchen?" Mom asked.

"No thank you. I'm going up to my room to play with Miss Kitty. She misses Mr. Kitty, so she's feeling kinda lonely. Call me when Daddy gets in. I want to tell him about class." Callie woolly wiggled up the stairs to her room.

She sat down on the window seat in her room to write a letter to Meghan. Miss Kitty was sleeping on her bed. The house was real quiet, just the way Callie liked it.

Dear Meg,

I'm sorry we had a fight while you were here. It's just so hard being away from everyone in Greenville. I miss you and Grandmama and Papa. I went to dance today, and guess what? There is a boy there. He dances all by himself in another room. It's strange. But have no fear, I'll find out who he is!

Well, Meghan, I have to go for now. Miss Kitty misses Mr. Kitty, too.

Write back real soon!

Love you always,
Callie Ann

Callie was about to put the letter in the envelope when the phone rang. "I'll get it!" Callie called.

"Hello?"

"Hello, Callie. This is Karen Baker. Did your mother ask you about the show on Monday?"

"Yes, Mom asked me. And I'd love to. What time?" Callie asked.

"Three-thirty," Miss Karen said. "Your class will be wearing poodle skirts. We have a few extra if you don't have one."

"Great, I'll see you Monday. 'Bye now. Thank you for asking me." Callie hung up the phone. Then she remembered something. "I can't believe I didn't ask who the boy with red hair is!" she moaned to Miss Kitty.

"Callie, your daddy's home," Daddy called from the steps. "Your mom said you wanted to tell me something."

"Oh, Daddy, you wouldn't believe what kind of day I had. First, Meg's mom came early. And then Meg and I had a little fight—well, not really a fight. But, Daddy, she's changed so much! She don't even like fishing anymore." Callie said it all at once.

"Slow down, Callie. And it's *doesn't* like, not *don't* like," he said gently. "Honey, people change. Even Meghan. Look at me. I really used to enjoy playing softball, but now with my bad knee, well, I don't like to play as much. You've changed, too. When you were younger, you didn't want to say your prayers at night. You said you'd do it in the morning when God was awake. Remember that?" He pulled Callie close for a hug.

"Yeah, I remember. It made sense to me at the time," Callie said, half laughing. "Now I know God is always there and awake no matter when. I can even pray outside. David told me that."

"And you listened to your brother? Wow, I'm impressed. Now, what did you want to tell me about ballet class?" Daddy asked. Miss Kitty had jumped up to look out the window. Daddy scratched her behind the ears.

"OH YEAH!" Callie said loudly. "There is a BOY in the class—well, not in my class, but in the school. And he dances all by himself in another room. His hair is the same color as mine." Callie stopped to take a breath, then said, "I'm

going to find out who he is—and why he's dancing all by himself."

"Well, I'm sure you will," Daddy said. "Mom
also said you'd be dancing at the nursing home
on Monday. I was thinking that if you'd like, I
could meet you there. We can all go out to eat
when the show is over. We haven't done much
of that since we moved here."

"I'd love to, Daddy. Do you think we could
ask Jason if he wants to go with us?" Callie asked
as she danced around the room.

"A *boy*? Oh my, what is the world coming to?"
Daddy laughed. "Sure. See? That's another way
you've changed. When we moved in, you didn't
even want to talk to him. And now look at you.
You'll even eat with him."

"Oh, Daddy, stop teasing! After all, you're a
boy! You told me so yourself." Callie smiled. She
sure was lucky to have both her mom and dad.
Meghan had been really little when her daddy
died. Now it was just her mom and her.

"OK, Missy, then it's out for supper on Monday. I'll leave it to you to ask Jason. Make sure
you have his mom call us to say it's all right."
Daddy left Callie's room. "Oh, and by the way,

do you think you could make your bed? Or do we have to call the bed patrol in on you?"

"No problem, Daddy. I just forgot with all that went on today. I'll do it now." Callie pulled the sunflower quilt off the floor where she and Meghan had left it that morning. "Daddy?"

"Yes, sweetie?"

"I love you!" Callie flashed her dad a huge grin.

"Well, I love you bunches and bunches," her daddy said as he ran back in to tickle her. This was a game they always used to play in Greenville before Callie went to bed. It was really Callie's way to stay up a little longer, and her daddy knew it. He played along until Mom came in to calm both of them down.

"OK, OK, I give in. I'll clean my room now. I really do love you, Daddy," Callie tried to say. She was still laughing.

Daddy bent over to pick up the pillows they had knocked on the floor during the tickle match. "I love you, too, Miss Callie Ann," he said.

Chapter Five

Callie finished making her bed just as her mom came into the room.

"It sounded like you two have been at it again," Mom said. She looked around the clean room and smiled. "I haven't heard that kind of racket since we left Greenville."

"Sorry, Mom, but Daddy started it!" Callie ran down the stairs giggling, her dad right behind her.

As she flew out the back door, Callie saw Jason was home. "Hi, Jason! I can't talk now. Daddy is after me!"

"What did you do?" Jason started chasing after Callie, too.

"Nothing, he's just getting old and needs to

run," Callie called loudly enough for her daddy to hear.

"OLD! Miss Callie, you'd really better run now," Daddy called after her. "When I catch you, I'm going to tickle you to pieces!"

"Man, she really can run." Jason stopped chasing her and sat on the steps of the back porch next to Mom. He tried to catch his breath.

"I'm just glad to see her back to her old self," Mom said. "She and her daddy used to do this all the time in Greenville. Now I guess you could say Callie is really home."

"Watch what you say. I can hear you!" Callie yelled as she and her daddy zipped by.

"Time! Enough, Callie," Daddy gasped. "You're right, I'm too old for this." He sat down on the steps, breathing hard.

"OK, Daddy. It's too hot to be running any-way," Callie said, plopping down beside him. "Oh, Jason, my ballet class is putting on a show at the nursing home on Monday. Then my family is going out to eat. Wanna come with us?"

"I'll have to ask Mom, but I think it'll be all right with her," Jason answered as he picked up Miss Kitty. "Boy, are you fat."

"She's not fat! She's just a big cat." Callie pulled Miss Kitty away from Jason.

"Well, excuse me. She looks even bigger now than when y'all moved in," Jason replied, picking up Jack. "Jack is getting fat, too. But all he does is eat and sleep."

"Callie, remember you wanted to ask Jason something," Mom reminded Callie as she got up to go in the house with Daddy.

"What did you want to ask me, Callie? Do you want to know if I like Meghan?" Jason teased.

"Get real, Jason. It's nothing like that. I went to ballet class today," Callie explained. "And I saw a boy at the school. He was dancing in a room all by himself. Do you know any boys who take dance?"

"Most of the boys I know wouldn't be caught dead around the ballet school. What did he look like?" Jason asked as they walked around the house to the pecan tree.

"I'm not sure. I really didn't get a good look at him, except for his red hair. He's small, but then again, so is the Mason boy, and he's our age. I don't know how old he is." Callie sat on a low branch of the old tree.

"Great, here we go again. I guess you want me to follow him like I did your mom," Jason called down. Callie had asked him to spy on her mom the week before. She had wanted to find out what the plans were for her birthday.

Jason climbed to a branch high in the tree. "You really should clean your room, Callie. I can see in, and it's a mess."

"It is not, Jason Alexander. I just cleaned it! Now stop looking in my room and help me think of boys who might take ballet!" she yelled up into the tree.

"Sorry, but I really don't know any boys who take ballet. Besides, why do you want to know who he is? Are you leaving me for someone else?" Jason pretended he was hurt and put his hand over his heart.

"Jason, you had better get down here right now, or I'll have to come up and hurt you," Callie warned in a loud voice.

"Oh, all right, Callie. Can't you take a joke? You've been in a bad mood ever since Meghan went home. What's going on with you?" Jason backed partway down the tree.

"Nothing really. It's just that . . . well, Meghan

has changed a lot. And now I feel like we're not best friends anymore," Callie answered sadly.

"You always have me. Good old Jason. Who else can you get to spy on people?" Then he lowered his voice. "You want me to ask about the boy at church in the morning?"

"Would you? Oh, Jason, you really are a friend!" Callie shouted almost at the top of her lungs.

"Maybe when I grow up, I'll have a job as a spy," Jason said, smiling. Then he climbed all the way down to the ground. "I've got to go eat now. See you later."

"OK, I'll see you at church tomorrow," Callie called as she rushed to pick up Miss Kitty. She didn't want the big black cat to climb into the pecan tree.

Inside, Callie and Miss Kitty went up to Callie's room. "What was Jason talking about? My room is clean. Boys!" Callie laughed as she put Miss Kitty in the window seat. "Miss Kitty, who do you think that little boy is? Maybe he's a spy for Miss Karen's other ballet school!"

"Suppertime, Miss Callie Ann. Come on down," Daddy broke in.

"Coming, Daddy. You stay here, Miss Kitty. I'll be back as soon as I'm done. Don't go under the bed again. You know how hard it is to get you out." Callie petted the cat, who was now curled up and purring.

All during supper, Callie talked about the little red-haired boy. She asked everyone who they thought he was. But no one had any idea.

◈◈◈

As soon as Callie and David finished with the dishes, Callie went back into her room. For some reason, she was very tired tonight. "Miss Kitty, I think I'll go take a bath. Then you and I will go to bed early." Callie pulled her nightgown out of her dresser. Inside her gown, she found a letter from Meghan.

"Look, Miss Kitty. Meghan must have put the letter in here while I was in the kitchen." Callie opened the letter.

Dear Callie,

I'll be at home by the time you find this, but I didn't want to leave with you mad at me. We have been friends for a

*long time. I guess seeing you with a new
friend upset me some. I know you'll make
new friends at school, and you and I
won't get to talk to each other every day.
But you are* still *my best friend in the
whole world. I'll miss you like crazy! I'll
write soon. Good luck at ballet class.*

> *Love you lots,*
> *Meg*

P.S. I really do like Jason (Ha Ha).

Callie laughed as she read the letter again.
Well, Meghan would always be her best friend,
too. But there was still room for more new
friends.

"Miss Kitty, I think it's time to take a bath and
go to bed. What do you say?" Callie asked the
cat, who was now lying upside down at the foot
of the bed.

Callie quickly took her bath. She was ready
for bed when her dad knocked on the door.
"You OK? We didn't see much of you after supper," Daddy said as he came into Callie's room.

"I'm just tired," she answered. "Daddy, is it
all right to pray for someone to always be your

best friend? I just want Meghan and me to always be friends."

"Well, Callie, I think it would be all right to pray that Meghan always stays a part of your life and that you can always be a part of hers. Sometimes people grow apart because of where their lives take them. But that doesn't mean you can't always think of them and remember them in your prayers." Daddy smiled and hugged Callie good-night.

After he left Callie's room, she sat down to read Meghan's letter again. What if she really did like Jason? What if she only came to visit so she could see Jason? "Oh, enough, Callie!" she told herself.

She knelt beside her bed to pray while Miss Kitty purred in her face. "Stop, Miss Kitty. You're tickling my nose." She brushed the cat's furry tail away from her face.

"Dear God, I'm kinda tired tonight, so this will be a short prayer. But Daddy said it doesn't matter how long we pray, just so we say our prayers. So here goes.

"Please bless Grandmama and Papa. Bless Meghan and Mrs. Johnson, Mom and Daddy and

David, Jason and his mom and dad.

"Oh, and God, could you help me find out who that little boy is at ballet? He dances like angels are guiding him, real light on his feet. Anyway, good night, God. Thank you for all my blessings. Amen."

Callie got into the bed and pulled Miss Kitty up next to her. "Good night, Miss Kitty, I love you, too." Callie pulled the sunflower quilt over her and fell sound asleep.

Chapter Six

"Get up, sleepyhead. It's time to get ready for church." Mom gently brushed Callie's hair out of her face.

"Good morning," Callie yawned as she rubbed the sleep out of her eyes. "I had a really strange dream last night. I dreamed I couldn't find that little boy. He was gone, and I never did get to see who he was."

Mom laughed. "This one has you over a barrel, doesn't it? I'm sure you'll find out soon enough. Now get up and put on your robe so you can come help me with breakfast."

"I need to wake up Miss Kitty and take her out first," Callie answered as she pulled the sleepy cat from under the quilt. "Boy, you sure like to sleep under the covers."

Mom was already starting breakfast when Callie and Miss Kitty came into the kitchen. Callie put Miss Kitty outside and pulled up the bright green stool to help her mom make pancakes. *I really love Sunday morning before church,* Callie thought. *Nobody else around but Mom and me.* She and her Mom always had a good time making Sunday's breakfast together.

"Mom, I just don't get it," Callie said as she began mixing up the second batch of batter. "The little boy was there one minute, and the next he was gone. I really want you to see him. He dances really good. He must have been taking ballet for a long time."

"Well, you'll find out tomorrow. You have to be at class around two-thirty. You can ask someone then." Mom put the first batch of pancakes on a warm plate.

"I don't know if I can wait that long. This is killing me." Callie put her hand to her forehead.

"What's killing you?" David asked as he came in the back door.

"Where have you been?" Callie said, looking at David funny. "You never get up this early unless you're going over to Jenni's."

"I've been running with Jenni and her friend Steven," David called as he backed out the door to pull off his running shoes. "Now, what's killing you?"

"Oh, I started ballet yesterday. There's a boy in the school—"

David grabbed his heart and fell to the floor. "A BOY! Oh my goodness, Callie, what are you going to do?" he teased. "You can't let a *boy* in your class."

"Enough, David, just listen," Mom warned.

"Anyway, as I was saying before someone had a *cow*, the boy dances in a room all by himself. He's real small and has red hair just like mine. He dances real well, too. I just have to know who he is." Callie put her pancakes on a small plate.

"Oh, I'm sure you'll find out who he is. You're good at spying on people," David called from the stairs. "Got to shower now."

"Mom," Callie said as she started to eat. "Did it make you mad that I was spying on you last week? If I did, I'm real sorry."

"No, you didn't make me mad. Sometimes

we just have to keep a secret for a while." Mom hugged Callie tightly. "Now, you go get dressed for church while I clean up this mess."

"Love you," Callie called back as she ran up the stairs.

Once up in her room, Callie started thinking. What if she never did find out who the boy was? What if she really hadn't seen him? After all, she hadn't gotten a lot of sleep while Meghan was visiting. *Well, I guess I'll have to wait until tomorrow to find out if I dreamed him or not.*

❧❧❧

Jason met Callie in the parking lot at church. He looked as though he may have discovered something.

"Callie, come quick!" Jason yelled as Callie got out of the family car. "Have I got something to show you."

Callie ran to meet Jason. "Did you find out who he is?"

"What? Who are you talking about?" Jason looked confused. "You mean the boy at ballet class? No, I didn't. But look what I found. A snakeskin." Jason proudly held up his find.

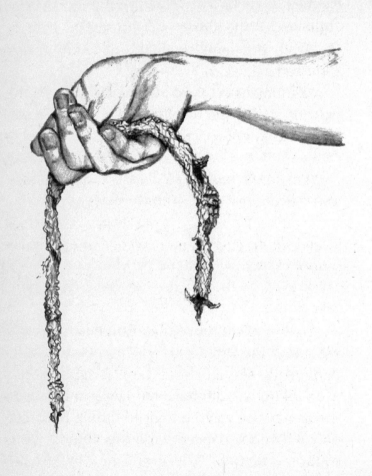

"A snakeskin? I thought you'd found out who the boy was. Who cares about snakeskins?" Callie said as she turned back toward the church.

"Well, the snake that lost it cared!" Jason shouted back. "Girls!"

Callie met her mom and daddy outside the pastor's study. She told them about the snakeskin and how Jason thought it was such a big deal.

"I'm sure it was a big deal to Jason," Daddy said. "Even if you didn't think so."

"You really are a boy, Daddy," Callie answered as she and her mom went to their Sunday school classes.

❧❦❧❦❧

All during church, Callie couldn't stop thinking about the mystery boy. There wasn't anything really special about the way he looked—even though he did have red hair just like hers. It was just the way he danced. Callie had seen only a few boy dancers. And this little boy was by far the best.

Looking around, Callie spotted Emilee Brown and her family. "Mom," Callie whispered,

"I'll ask Emilee about the boy after church. She's in my ballet class, so she's sure to know who he is."

"That's fine, Callie. Now be quiet," Mom whispered back, patting Callie on the leg.

But Callie could hardly wait until her daddy was through preaching. It seemed like this service was taking forever. And she was getting a bad case of the woolly wiggles.

As soon as Daddy said the last prayer, Callie started toward the door. She could see Emilee far ahead of her. But there were so many people, she couldn't move very fast. *I have to catch her before she leaves,* Callie thought.

Callie fought through the crowd to get to where she thought Emilee was. But when she got there, Emilee was gone! *Where did she disappear to?* Callie wondered.

Chapter Seven

Callie made her way through the crowd again to the church's front door. She got there just in time to see Emilee and her family pulling out of the parking lot.

"Oh, great!" Callie said out loud.

"Why, thank you, Miss Callie. I thought it was a nice service, too," Daddy said as he shook her hand. "Where's your mom?"

"She's over there talking to Mrs. Alexander. I think they're planning to go up to the mall in Statesville this afternoon," Callie said.

"Hey, Callie, do you want to eat with us?" Jason asked as he walked up to the steps of the church. "Dad told me to come and get Mom so we can go out."

"I don't think so, Jason. Mom put on a roast before we left home, and I love her pot roast." Callie twirled on the steps. "Can you play after y'all get back from eating?"

"I guess. Mom or Dad didn't say we were going anywhere else. I'll see you later, then," Jason said. He went into the church to get his mom.

"See ya." Callie turned back to her daddy. "Can we go now? I'm getting hungry, and Mom's roast is calling me."

"Ah yes, I think I do hear it calling your name." Daddy laughed and picked up Callie. "Let's go get your mom."

❧❧❧

Callie could smell the roast cooking as they came in the back door of the house. It reminded her of their house in Greenville. Grandmama always cooked Sunday dinner, and it always made the house smell so good. Callie decided to ask Mom if they could call Grandmama after they ate.

"Mom, are you and Mrs. Alexander going to the mall in Statesville this afternoon?" Callie asked as she piled her plate high with mashed potatoes and gravy.

"We were thinking about it. There's a craft show up there, and we need ideas for our craft bazaar at church in the fall." Mom was cutting up the roast. "Why? Do you and Jason want to go with us?"

"Not really. I was just going to ask if we could call Grandmama this afternoon," Callie answered.

"Sure we can. We'll have to call Aunt Debbie's. Grandmama and Grandpapa are over there eating dinner for your uncle's birthday," Mom said. "We can even sing 'Happy Birthday' on the phone."

"Great, I forgot today was Uncle Danny's birthday. Did you remember to send a card?" Callie asked, setting her full plate on the table.

"Sure did. I mailed it on Friday. And your daddy called the bakery in Greenville and had a cake sent to Grandmama's so she could take it over today for dinner," Mom said.

"Mom, did you ask anybody this morning about the boy at Miss Karen's?" Callie asked.

"No, honey. You said you were going to ask

Emilee," Mom answered.

"Well, I didn't make it outside before they left today. I guess I'll just have to wait." Callie sat down beside her daddy.

Before they started to eat, Daddy said the blessing.

"David, what are you going to do this afternoon?" Mom asked when Daddy was finished.

"I think I'll track down the mystery boy so I can see who he is," David said with a silly smile at Callie. "Then Jenni and I wanted to watch a movie that her dad has about whales."

"That's good." Then Mom turned to Callie. "And, Callie, what are you up to today?" she asked.

"Well, Jason and I were going to play or ride our bikes, if that's OK with you. I really don't want to go to Statesville," Callie answered.

"That's fine. Your daddy will be here. And David will be at Jenni's. Just remember not to get too dirty. We have to be back at church this evening around six-thirty," Callie's mom said.

"GREAT!" Callie yelled.

"I've never known you to be excited about

going back to church on Sunday night," Daddy said, laughing.

"It's great because maybe Emilee will be there. I want to ask her about the boy." Callie grinned. "Not that I don't love going to hear you, Daddy. It's just that I hear you all the time."

"Oh, great, Cal. I think you'd better stop while you're ahead," David said. "I'll tell you what. I'll ask Jenni's mom. She's a teacher in your school. Maybe she knows him. OK?"

"Would you, David? You're the best!" Callie jumped up to hug him.

"Man, you really must want to know who this person is," David said.

"Yeah, I really do. You should see him dance. It's almost like he has angels pulling him along. I've never seen a boy dance the way he was," Callie said in a low voice. "I know he must have been taking ballet for a while. The dance he was doing was from the *Nutcracker*. We did it last year in Greenville. It's hard."

"Well, I'll see what Jenni's mom knows. She teaches the grade above yours. Maybe she'll be your teacher next year," David said as Callie danced around the kitchen to put her dishes in the sink.

"I'm sure I'd like her. I like Jenni a lot." Callie flashed a huge smile at David. "You like Jenni a lot, too, don't you, Mr. David Paul Davies?"

"Callie, I'm not going to let you bother me. After all, I'm not the one who is dying to know who a certain little boy is at her ballet school," he answered smugly.

"OK, you two, that's enough." Mom put a stop to their teasing. "Callie, you need to change out of your good dress if you and Jason are going riding. And, David, if you're planning to go to Jenni's house, you have to take the trash out and clean your room first."

Upstairs in David's room, David asked Callie, "Did you and Meg have a good time while she was here?"

"Yeah, I guess," Callie answered.

"You don't seem too sure," David said. "Want to talk about it?" He plopped on his unmade bed.

"David, you had to leave all your friends in Greenville, but you seem to be fine with it. Why do I have such a hard time finding new friends?"

Callie asked from the spot she had taken on the floor.

"I don't think you've had a hard time finding new friends, Callie. Jason is a good friend. And y'all have a good time riding your bikes and all. Now that you're going to ballet class, you'll meet girls who'll be your friends, too," David said.

"I guess. But didn't it bother you to have to leave all your friends when we moved here?" Callie looked around David's room. Now she knew why Mom wanted him to clean it before he went over to Jenni's.

"Sure it did. I mean, I've been in school with the same people for years. And I do miss them and Grandmama and Papa a lot. But this is what we had to do, so I write letters to all of them and stuff. I make the best of it." David stood up. "Want to help me clean my room?" He gave her a big grin.

"NO THANK YOU!" Callie answered loudly. "I'll pass on that one."

Chapter Eight

Miss Kitty was coming up the steps when Callie went into her room. "Well, where have you been?" Callie asked.

Miss Kitty just meowed and hopped up on the bed to take her afternoon nap. Yawning and rolling over so her belly was up to the cool air of the fan, she looked like a black pool in the middle of Callie's bed.

"Have a good nap, Miss Kitty," Callie said while she rubbed the cat's belly. "You really *are* getting big."

The phone rang, and Callie jumped up. "I wonder who that is? Maybe it's someone to tell me who that little boy is. Or maybe it's Grand-mama."

"Callie, phone. It's Jason," Daddy called up the steps to Callie's room. "And if we're going to call Grandmama, we need to do that as soon as you get off the phone, OK?"

"OK, Daddy, I'll just talk a few minutes," Callie yelled back. "Hello, Jason. Are y'all back from eating?"

"Yeah, I'll be out in a little while," Jason said. "I have to make my bed first and help Dad take out the trash. Can you come out then?"

"I think so. We're going to call my Grandmama in Greenville and talk to her for a few minutes. And I have to wish my Uncle Danny happy birthday. Then I can." Callie looked at the now snoring Miss Kitty.

"OK. I'll see you outside," Jason replied. " 'Bye."

Callie patted Miss Kitty to make her stop snoring, then she went down to tell Mom and Daddy that she was off the phone.

"Great, we'll call your uncle now," Mom said. She stood up to get the phone. "Do you want to sing 'Happy Birthday' to him, Callie?"

"I guess. But I'm not a good singer," Callie reminded her.

"I'm sure Uncle Danny won't mind if we're off key," Daddy said as he pulled Callie into his lap. "You just sing real loud so he can't hear me. OK, sweetie?"

"All right, Daddy. I'll sing real loud, but you won't like it." Callie smiled sweetly at her daddy. She'd start singing, then stop and let Daddy carry it all. He had a great voice.

Just as Callie had planned, her daddy ended up singing to her uncle all by himself. Callie giggled. "That was great, Daddy."

She was the first one to talk to Grandmama and Uncle Danny. "Hope you have a great birthday, Uncle Danny. Tell everybody hello and that I miss them," Callie said, holding back tears as she handed the phone to Daddy.

"Mom, can I go out now?" she asked.

"Sure, honey. I'll call you when Mrs. Alexander and I get ready to go to Statesville," Mom said.

Callie went out the back door and around to the old pecan tree. There, as always, was Jason. At least this time he wasn't at the top of the tree. Instead he was lying on his back in the grass.

"Whatcha doing?" Callie asked.

"Waiting on you. What took you so long?" Jason asked as he sat up.

"I talked to everybody in Greenville," Callie said. "Did you know that our moms are going to the mall?"

"Yeah. Mom said I didn't have to go if I didn't want to. How about you? Do you have to go?" Jason asked. He had climbed into the tree and was swinging upside down.

"No. Mom said I could stay home with Daddy," Callie said. "Move over so I can get up in the tree, too. Did you ask anybody at church about that boy?"

Jason moved to another branch of the tree and started swinging on it. "Yeah," he said. "I asked Bobby and Steve, and they don't know any boys with red hair who take ballet. Did you ask Emilee?"

"I didn't have time. By the time I got to the parking lot, her family was gone. I guess I'll have to ask tonight when we go back to church," Callie said.

"You might not have time. Remember, our Sunday school class is helping to take care of the

babies tonight. And Emilee isn't in our class," Jason reminded Callie.

"Oh no! Is that tonight? I can't believe I forgot that. Maybe I can get Mom to ask her. I don't want to have to wait until tomorrow to find out." Callie was down in the dumps now.

"Look at it this way, Cal," Jason said. "It's already four-thirty. We have to be at church at six-thirty, so you won't have much time to think about it. Then it'll be tomorrow."

Callie and Jason sat under the pecan tree the rest of the afternoon. Jack played with the pecans that had fallen from the tree.

When it was almost time for Callie to get ready for church, she asked Jason again, "Are you *sure* you don't know who I'm talking about? You're not just making me wait until tomorrow, are you?" Callie wasn't sure she should believe him.

"C'mon, Callie, I'm not mean," Jason said. "Boy, when you get on to something, you just won't let go. I mean, I didn't know anything about your party, but you wouldn't stop asking about it. So I helped you find out what I could.

And now I'll help you find out about this mystery boy of yours."

"OK. I'm sorry. I guess I do get caught up in things." Callie got up to leave. "See you at church."

❀❀❀

Once she was at church, Callie had her hands full helping out with the babies. The Hoover twins were running all over the place. So was the little VanHoy girl.

"Jason, I'm so tired! Babies are a lot of work," Callie said, falling into a chair in the corner of the room.

"I know. I can't believe anybody would want to have a baby. I think anyone who wants one should have to work in here for a day," Jason replied

"Yeah, I do, too," Callie said. "Oh, I didn't get to see Emilee before church. I'm going to try to catch her after the service." Just then the Hoover twins zipped by. Callie jumped up and ran after them before they went down the steps.

❀❀❀

When the church service was over, Callie saw Emilee coming her way. *Great,* she thought. *Now I can ask her if she knows the little boy.* But before she could get to Emilee, Mrs. VanHoy stopped Callie to tell her that Yvonne had a wonderful time with her in the nursery.

"Thank you, Mrs. VanHoy. She was a very good girl tonight," Callie said, looking around to see where Emilee went.

She found Jason instead. "Jason, did you see Emilee? I was talking to Mrs. VanHoy when I saw her. Now I can't find her."

"Yeah. I saw her leave with her mom. You didn't get to talk to her?" Jason asked.

"No, I didn't. Now I really will have to wait," Callie grumbled.

"Well, at least it's not as long now as it was," Jason said. "I gotta go. Mom and Dad are ready. See you in the morning." He waved as he went to join his parents.

❧❧❧

All the way home, Callie kept thinking about who the boy might be.

"I can't believe I didn't catch Emilee at

church," Callie told her mom when they were home. "I know she could have told me."

"You'll find out soon enough who the boy is, Callie," Daddy said. "It's time to get ready for bed now. Good night."

"Good night, Daddy," Callie said as she went upstairs.

"Miss Kitty, move over. I need to get in bed, too," Callie told the big cat. "Over to one side, please."

Callie climbed into her soft bed. Looking around, she thought, *I really do like my new room. And I even like Jason as a friend. But I still miss Greenville.*

Chapter Nine

Monday started out rainy, so Callie called Jason. Maybe he would want to play a board game on the back porch or something.

"Sure, Callie. I'd like that. What time do you have to go to dance?" Jason asked.

"Around two. Why?" Callie answered.

"Mom wanted to know what time we'd be leaving," Jason said. "I'll be over in a minute."

"OK," Callie said and hung up the phone. She ran downstairs to tell her mom that Jason was on his way.

"Maybe he can find out who the boy is for you while you're dancing," Mom suggested.

Jason ran onto the back porch just as it

started raining really hard. "Boy, I just made it," he said.

"Hey, Jason, while I'm at dance, maybe you could find out who the boy is," Callie said.

"I'll try, but how am I going to know where to look?" he asked. He pulled a game out of the old trunk that used to be Callie's great-uncle's.

"I can show you the room he was in, and you can ask questions. OK?" Callie answered.

"OK. I'll do what I can. But I might not be able to find out much," Jason said.

They spent the early afternoon on the porch playing games and talking. Callie asked Jason all about school and how he came from England to the United States. She talked about anything to keep her mind off the dance class and the little boy. The rain didn't stop until it was almost time to leave for Statesville.

"You two ready?" Mom asked as she pulled on her raincoat. "Callie, you had better get your jacket so you don't get too wet. Jason, do you want a jacket, too?" She held out a jacket of David's.

"Yes ma'am, thank you," Jason said, taking the jacket. Wearing it made him look small.

All the way to Statesville, Callie was quiet. She was thinking of ways to ask people who the red-haired boy was. Why was he dancing all alone in a room?

Before she could figure it all out, they were there.

"You hurry ahead, Callie. We're a few minutes late because of the rain," Mom said as she pulled into a parking space.

Callie ran in the door just in time. They were starting the first dance they were going to do at Sunset Nursing Home. She quickly took off her raincoat and put it on a chair by the door.

"Good to see you, Callie. I'm sure you know this number," Miss Karen called to her as Callie put her shoes on. "It's one you danced in Greenville."

Callie looked all around, but there was no boy in sight. *I know I wasn't dreaming him up,* she thought to herself.

Everything went so fast that Callie didn't even have time to show Jason the room the boy had been in. Miss Karen kept them busy until it was time to put on their costumes and go to the nursing home.

"All right now, girls, listen up. This is really nice of y'all to do this as a treat for the folks at Sunset. I'm sure they will love y'all. Now, Mrs. Davies will be driving some of you, and I'll be driving the rest. So let's go and make some people happy." Miss Karen pulled her raincoat off the coat hook.

"Great, I'll get to ask some of the girls riding with us who the boy with the red hair is," Callie told her mom and Jason as they went to the car.

Miss Karen came running to the car just as they got in. "Mrs. Davies, thank you for offering to drive, but Natalie's mom is here. She has a van, so we'll all just ride with her. Y'all can follow us over, OK?"

"That will be just fine," Mom said. She looked back at Callie. "Sorry, honey, but I guess you won't get to ask after all."

Callie rolled her eyes. "I *will* ask somebody who he is before I leave the nursing home," she vowed.

Chapter Ten

Sunset Nursing Home was only about two blocks from the dance school. It was a big green building with a huge porch that went all the way around it. *There must be fifty rocking chairs*, Callie thought as she went up the walk lined with all kinds of pretty flowers.

"Hurry, Callie," Miss Karen called to her from the door. "I need y'all in your places."

Callie hurried in and up the hall to a big room with lots of chairs and tables in it. There were some old people playing games and watching TV. Some of them looked like they were asleep. *Well, not for long,* she thought. *We'll wake 'em up.*

"OK, girls, now take your places. As soon as Miss Black gets in, we'll start," Miss Karen said.

"I know y'all are going to be great. And y'all look so cute in your poodle skirts! I want to get a picture before we leave today so I can show my other classes. Now, quiet. Here she comes." Miss Karen turned to meet with Miss Black.

"All right, girls, it's show time. Smile real big and do well," Miss Karen said as she walked back on stage where the girls were standing.

"Ladies and gentlemen, we'd like to thank you for having us dance for you today. We hope you like our little show. This is my most advanced class. They do a wonderful job," Miss Karen told all the people who were now in the room.

Before the music started, Callie looked around and saw that her daddy had arrived. He was sitting with her mom and Jason. Callie looked behind them—and there he was! The boy with red hair was sitting right behind her parents and Jason!

I can't believe this, Callie thought. *I can't even tell them that he's behind them!*

The girls danced to four songs, and the people loved it. Many of them moved along with the music. Some of them even got up and danced around. Callie tried to keep an eye on the little boy, but she lost sight of him. *Why me?* she

thought. *All I want to do is to know who he is and why he was dancing by himself.*

When the last song was almost over, she saw him again. But this time he was behind the curtain next to the stage. Was he going to dance?

Miss Karen came out on stage. "Thank you for having us. Thank you, too, for dancing along with us. We really loved it. Girls, you may go sit with your parents."

All the girls went off the stage and sat with their moms and dads. As soon as Callie got to her mom, she asked if she had seen the little boy with the red hair sitting right behind them.

"No, honey, I didn't. I was watching you and the others. Is he still here?" Mom asked.

"Yeah, but he's backstage now. I think he's going to dance," Callie said in a low voice.

Miss Karen was still up on stage waiting for the rest of the girls to find a seat. When they were all in place, she started talking again. "We have a very special person at our school—not that all our young people are not special. But this one is very special to me because he was my first student. He and I have been through a lot together. His name is Sean Thompson. Sean cannot hear.

He was born deaf. When he was three, his mom and dad asked if I could teach him ballet to help with his balance. I can truly tell you that he needed no help from me. Sean has a wonderful gift. He dances like no one I have ever seen."

The whole time Miss Karen was talking, Callie could see someone signing to the boy backstage. *That's who he is!*

"But how can he dance if he can't hear?" Callie asked without thinking.

"Well, to answer your question, Callie—and it is a good question," Miss Karen said, "Sean can feel the vibration of the music in his feet. He counts off steps. That's why he dances so well. He always has to count his steps. I'd like for all of you to watch with me as Sean does a piece from the *Nutcracker*."

Everyone watched Sean as he jumped and twirled. "Look at him, Mom. He's wonderful." Callie smiled. "I told you he dances like angels are with him. Just look!"

When Sean finished, everyone stood up to clap for him. Callie was still clapping when they all sat back down.

Miss Karen called all the girls back to the

stage to take a bow, and Sean stayed on with them. Callie could not believe that someone who couldn't hear could dance so wonderfully.

When the clapping was over, Callie went up to Miss Karen and took her hand. "Miss Karen, I saw Sean the other day at the school. And I've been trying to find out who he is and why he was dancing all by himself. Now I know. He's wonderful. I wish I could dance as well as he does."

"Well, Callie, you dance as well as Sean. He's been at it a long time, but he had a lot to overcome. It's hard to dance when you can't hear," Miss Karen explained as they walked to meet Sean.

"I feel sorry for him," Callie said.

"Well, you shouldn't," Miss Karen answered back quickly. "Sean is very good at what he does. The fact that he can't hear doesn't mean you need to feel sorry for him. He does well in school, and he has a very full life. Did you know that Sean is the same age you are? But he's in the sixth grade. He's very smart. So you don't have to feel sorry for him. He's doing great."

"I never looked at it that way. I guess people like Sean don't really want us to feel sorry for them. We should just treat them like they're one of us—'cause they are!" Callie said, smiling.

❧❦❧

On the way to the restaurant and all through supper, Callie told everyone about meeting Sean. She talked about how she could talk to him through an interpreter who knew sign language. And she talked about how Sean was in sixth grade and how he played ball and did all the things that other kids did.

"Sounds like you really liked Sean," Jason said, sounding a little put out. Was he jealous that Callie was talking about another boy?

"I do, Jason. He's funny and signs jokes and all. But don't worry. I'm not trading you in just yet. You're still my buddy." Callie gave Jason one of her looks. She was up to something, and he'd be in on it soon enough.

The End

Series for Young Readers*
From Bethany House Publishers

★ ★ ★

THE ADVENTURES OF CALLIE ANN
by Shannon Mason Leppard

Readers will giggle their way through the true-to-life escapades of Callie Ann Davies and her many North Carolina friends.

★ ★ ★

BACKPACK MYSTERIES
by Mary Carpenter Reid

This excitement-filled mystery series follows the mishaps and adventures of Steff and Paulie Larson as they strive to help often-eccentric relatives crack their toughest cases.

★ ★ ★

THE CUL-DE-SAC KIDS
by Beverly Lewis

Each story in this lighthearted series features the hilarious antics and predicaments of nine endearing boys and girls who live on Blossom Hill Lane.

★ ★ ★

RUBY SLIPPERS SCHOOL
by Stacy Towle Morgan

Join the fun as home-schoolers Hope and Annie Brown visit fascinating countries and meet inspiring Christians from around the world!

★ ★ ★

THREE COUSINS DETECTIVE CLUB®
by Elspeth Campbell Murphy

Famous detective cousins Timothy, Titus, and Sarah-Jane learn compelling Scripture-based truths while finding—and solving—intriguing mysteries.

* (ages 7–10)

9611